For David Davies

First published 1985 by
Walker Books Ltd
184-192 Drummond Street
London NW1 3HP

© 1985 Shirley Hughes

First printed 1985
Reprinted 1986, 1987
Printed and bound by
L.E.G.O., Vicenza, Italy

British Library Cataloguing in Publication Data
Hughes, Shirley
When we went to the park. – (Nursery collection;2)
1. Numeration – Juvenile literature
I. Title II. Series
513'.2 QA141.3

ISBN 0-7445-0301-9

When We Went To The Park

Shirley Hughes

WALKER BOOKS
LONDON

When Grandpa and I put on our coats

and went to the park...

We saw one black cat sitting on a wall,

Two big girls licking ice-creams,

Three ladies chatting on a bench,

Four babies in buggies,

Five children playing in the sand-pit,

Six runners running,

Seven dogs chasing one another,

Eight boys kicking a ball,

Nine ducks swimming on the pond,

Ten birds swooping in the sky,

and so many leaves that I couldn't
count them all.

On the way back we saw the
black cat again.

Then we went home for tea.

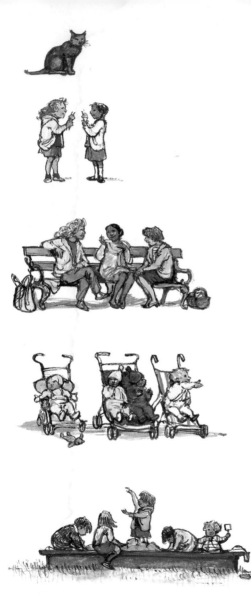